1980

To Alexander

TEN FAIRY TALES

Merry Christmas

Auntie Vera

TEN
FAIRY TALES

Retold by
Robert Sargent

Simon & Schuster
New York

For Mother

Published by Simon & Schuster, Inc., Children's Book Division
Rockefeller Center, 630 Fifth Avenue
New York, New York 10020

First Printing

Library of Congress Catalog Card Number: 68 - 29759
Manufactured in the United States of America
Printed by Reehl Litho., Inc.

Contents

The Magic Wart

Long ago, in a land far off in the eastern part of the world, the farmers were being plagued by witches that lived in the nearby forests. It seemed that the witches made so much noise at night that the farmers' animals weren't able to get their proper sleep.

The farmers decided therefore to get together and devise a plan to capture the witches.

On the afternoon that all the farmers came together to talk about what to do about the witches, a little boy who was the son of one of the farmers came to listen, too.

"We should set a trap and capture them," one farmer said.

"They kept my chickens up all night last week," said another.

"We should burn the forest down," cried another, but after much discussion the farmers agreed that the forest couldn't be burned down because they needed the wood for building barns. Finally, they decided that setting a trap for the witches would be the best plan.

When the boy returned home to his mother, she asked him what the farmers had decided to do. The boy told her that they would all get together in a few days and trap the witches in the forest.

"Well, the witches never hurt anyone," his mother declared, "but of course they are noisy and I guess that is the only way to stop it."

"What do witches look like?" asked the boy.

"Well, I have seen only two in my life," said his mother,

"and that was a long time ago when I was a girl, but as I remember, they had long hair and skinny hands and there was always a wart someplace. Usually on their nose or cheek. They weren't the prettiest things that I've seen in life."

"I have a wart," said the boy, and he held his thumb knuckle up for his mother to see.

"Lots of people have those," said his mother. "That doesn't mean anything. It will go away in time."

But the more that the boy looked at it, the more he thought that it wasn't just an ordinary wart.

That night when he went to bed he began to wonder if perhaps his wart was really a witch's wart. In fact, perhaps he was part witch himself! He could hardly go to sleep!

Then about the middle of the night, he heard the howling and whooping of the witches' voices coming across the fields from the forest. He went to his window and tried to see if anything was moving over there, but it was much too dark and too far away to tell.

The next day when he had done all his chores, carrying in the wood for his mother's cooking and helping her to wash the breakfast dishes, and had put the hay down and fed the pigs, he walked up by the forest.

It was certainly dark in the forest. But the boy took a deep breath and, holding his shoulders very straight so that no one would ever think he was afraid, he marched in.

The forest was very still. The great trees creaked with overhanging branches that dragged on the ground. The tops of the trees were so thick that hardly a sliver of sunlight came through. The forest smelled wonderful though and the boy stopped worrying immediately.

When he realized that nothing was moving he decided that the best way would be to call out.

"Come out, witches," he called. "I know you're in here."

He called several times and still nothing moved and no answer came back.

So he called again, "Come out, witches! Don't be afraid! I'm part witch too!"

Still there was no sound. The forest seemed to be waiting.

Just as he was turning to go home, he heard a rustling in the bushes nearby and some whispering going on.

So he sat down and waited a little longer.

Eventually two timid witches appeared looking over the bushes at him! Then a third one slid down a tall pine tree. Then

a fourth, and a fifth and a sixth one arrived from the darkest corners of the forest.

"We're supposed to be sleeping," one complained.

"That's right," said another. "I hope that it's important because I had to leave a delicious dream about spiders."

"Oh it's important all right," said the boy.

"Who are you?" they all asked at the same time.

"I live over in the farmhouse beyond the field," said the boy. "But don't be afraid because I'm really part witch too."

"Part witch?!!" several cried in amazement.

"You don't look like a witch," said the tallest one.

"Prove it!" cried the short fat one.

"Yes, prove it!" the others cried.

Then the little boy held his hand up so they could all see his thumb knuckle.

"I have a wart, too," he said proudly.

"Hmmmn . . . " they all said, as they each took a turn bending over it and looking very carefully at it.

"It is a nice one," conceded one.

"Mine's larger!" sniffed one who had a wart on the end of her nose.

"But you are older, and I'm just a boy witch," said the boy.

"Don't talk about my age, please," growled the witch.

"Is it magical?" asked one of the witches shyly.

"What do you mean?" asked the boy.

"Can it do things?" asked another. "Witches' warts can always do things."

"I've never tried," said the boy.

"Well, try to wiggle it. Something should happen if it's magical," the friendliest one coaxed.

So the boy tried to wiggle his wart and then he tried waving it over his head, and then he rubbed it until it turned red, but nothing happened.

"There!" cried one witch. "An absolute fake! He doesn't even have a magical power!"

10

"What can yours do?" asked the boy.

"Everything!" they answered together. "That's what our warts are for!"

Then one of the witches wiggled her wart and a cloud of colorful butterflies flew from out of nowhere and circled around the boy's head turning different brilliant colors from rose, to blue, to yellow, to cinnamon to lavender to green! Then suddenly they all turned into little silver bells and when they had tinkled out a little song, they turned to snowflakes and, falling, melted on the ground!

The little boy had hardly caught his breath when the witch who had said that his wart was bigger smiled and rubbed it until it turned purple. Suddenly the tree beside the boy turned into a pile of chocolates and as he reached for one, it turned again to porcupine quills and then to soft little white mice with shiny eyes and then back to the tree that it was before!

"Could you make my wart have a magical power, too?" the little boy asked.

"Well," said one, "you would have to trade something for it. What have you got to trade? Witches love to bargain, you know."

The boy thought and thought. He hadn't brought anything with him. If he'd known that he had to bargain with the witches he could have brought a pig from the barn, but he hadn't planned on that.

"I didn't bring anything with me," said the boy sadly.

"Then we can't just give you a magical power!" snorted the tall witch. "Magical powers are very precious, you know!"

"Don't you have anything to trade?" asked the friendly one again.

The boy thought and thought but the answer was the same.

"No, I guess I just don't have," he said and he hung his head.

"If you don't have anything to trade," said one, "I'm going back to my wonderful dream about spiders."

Then the tall one asked, "Maybe you've heard some good stories? We all love stories."

11

But the boy couldn't remember anything that had really been so interesting to tell.

"Maybe you know a secret!" suggested the fat witch. "We witches will do anything for a secret."

Then the little boy smiled and said, "Yes, perhaps I know a secret that I could trade."

"Well, it better be an important one," growled one witch. "We just can't pass out magical powers for secrets that aren't important."

"Oh, this is very important!" exclaimed the boy.

The witches whispered to each other for a moment. Then the friendly one asked, "What is the thing that you dislike the most in all the world?"

The little boy thought and thought. It wasn't easy to say because he liked almost everything. Everything except going after the cows.

"I don't like going after the cows every night," he said.

Then the witch took the little boy's hand and sprinkled a pinch of dust over his wart.

"Now it is magical!" the witch said.

The others were becoming impatient.

"Tell us the secret!" they all cried at once.

Then the boy told the witches that he had been at a meeting with his father, and heard that the other farmers were planning to come into the forest to trap the witches because they made too much noise at night and kept the animals awake.

"Ooooooohhh!!!!" they all cried in surprise.

"We're the partying type. We just can't change our way of living because the cows and the hens don't like it," complained one witch nervously.

"That means we should move to another forest," agreed the fat one. "I never did like this place anyway."

They all talked at once.

Finally they turned to the boy.

"We'll move to another forest. It will be better for all of us," said the tall witch.

Then they thanked the boy for his secret, and turning, they floated out toward the dark ends of the forest.

"Good-bye," called the boy. "Thank you for making my wart magical!"

"Think nothing of it," the last witch called back.

The next day the farmers went into the forest to search out the witches and much to their surprise there wasn't a witch to be found. Furthermore from that time on witches were never heard about in that part of the countryside.

The boy went about his usual life on the farm, helping his father and his mother as he always did, bringing in the wood for the fire, putting down the hay, feeding the pigs and chickens, but one thing had changed.

Every afternoon about four o'clock, the boy would rub his thumb knuckle wart ever so gently, and without any explanation the cows would come home by themselves.

The Lonely Dragon

It was in the spring when the last dragon came out of his cave. He sniffed the air, stretched himself up to his full size, and then trotted down to the brook for a sip of cool, fresh water.

He had been the last dragon for some time. There wasn't another one around.

Throughout the winters he would sleep quietly, folded up in his cave, dreaming of the days long ago when dragons were the mightiest and bravest creatures on earth. But times had changed since then, and when he awoke each spring he always had to face the truth. Other dragons were definitely not to be found.

The other animals weren't very nervous about having just one dragon in the forest because he kept to himself most of the time and didn't bother them. He had even grown a little timid in his old age and if something surprised him along the path in the forest, he often jumped behind a rock and hid, or just folded himself up into a tiny little packet about the size of a leaf. He had been able to do this ever since he was a youngster. It was a talent which only the best dragons had.

When this happened you wouldn't be able to tell that there was a dragon nearby at all!

One thing that did disturb the dragon very much, when he thought about his quiet life in the forest, was that he wasn't important anymore and that he didn't belong to someone who took an interest in him.

15

Since he was a bit timid at heart, he really couldn't challenge anyone successfully either. So his days remained dull.

Now it happened that one afternoon when the leaves along the bank of the brook were drying in the warm sun, a lady who had been visiting her aunt in the farmhouse nearby was returning to her home in the village on the other side of the mountain, and she came along this path.

The dragon was gazing at his reflection in the water to keep from feeling lonely and realized, too late, that someone was approaching.

He hadn't time to hide behind a rock, so he quickly folded himself up into a tiny packet the size of a leaf and held his breath.

The lady had been picking flowers, so she had her arms full, but as she came nearer she saw the little packet.

She picked it up.

"I wonder what this is?" she said. "It feels like very old leather. It would make a nice hot plate for my coffeepot."

Then she opened her purse and dropped the small packet inside.

When she got home she put the flowers in a vase and then she remembered the little leather packet she had seen on the road.

So she took it out and laid it gently on the table.

It was the right size for her coffeepot!

"Now I won't burn the table again," she said happily.

She had some difficulty lighting the stove. The wood was still damp and there was no draft to make the flame catch. But eventually after much talking to it, the stove seemed to work.

She put the coffeepot on to boil.

The dragon was wondering where he was. He could hear someone talking and she sounded upset. He waited patiently. He could not see out when he was folded up.

Then the lady brought the coffeepot over and set it down on him.

When he felt the pot, he leaped off the table onto the floor!

The pot flew into the air! The lady jumped back!

Then the dragon unfolded himself.

"Who are you?!!" screamed the lady as she hid behind the sink.

"I'm a dragon," the dragon said.

"Oh dear! So you are! How did you get into my kitchen?" asked the lady nervously.

"You brought me here," replied the dragon.

The lady looked back at the table. She saw that the packet wasn't there anymore, and the dragon looked like the same leathery material.

"Oh dear! If I'd known that I had picked up a dragon I would have fainted a long time ago," she exclaimed.

"That's all right. I'm not bad-tempered," said the dragon, and he tried to smile. "I wouldn't have leaped up but your coffeepot tickled me."

17

The lady looked around rather nervously.

"Well, you'd better go back to wherever you came from. I can't have a dragon in my house!"

The dragon didn't know what to say. He felt sad. If he left now, he wouldn't have anything but a cave to go back to. It would be the same old way of life every day. He shuddered just thinking about it. But if he stayed here there would be someone to talk to and belong to.

So he said, "I heard you had trouble lighting your stove."

"Yes," said the lady. "It doesn't light well and the wood is usually too damp and the fire takes a long time in heating up the room. But I cannot afford a new stove."

Then the dragon said, "If I could be of help, I would be glad to stay on. I could be very useful. I could light your fires with my special breath and I could heat the room in the winter, and if you need a coffeepot insulator I could probably get used to that with a little practice."

The lady saw by the look in the dragon's eyes that he was trying to be friendly. She couldn't turn him away just because he was a dragon. Also she needed a watchdog, and with a dragon around she knew she would feel a lot safer and could sleep better.

"Well, if you're careful not to burn anything," she said.

"Oh, I'll be very careful," answered the dragon.

"And what will my friends say if they know that I've a dragon in my house?" she asked. "They will stay away, I'm afraid."

"They won't ever know," said the dragon, "because I'll fold myself up and be your coffeepot insulator when they come to visit."

The lady thought about it a little longer.

"You won't mind sleeping behind the woodbox?" she asked.

"Oh no!" exclaimed the dragon. "The caves have been rather uncomfortable lately. They haven't been drying out as they should and they are very drafty. This will be fine."

"Then I suppose we could try it for a while," the lady said finally.

The dragon was so happy that he almost forgot about being careful and let out a special flame that landed in the dishpan, evaporating all the water, filling the room with steam.

"Oh!" cried the lady. "Do be careful!"

"Sorry," replied the dragon.

The days after soon became well organized. The dragon lit the fires for the cooking in the morning and played watchdog at night. When the visitors came he folded up as a coffeepot insulator, resting on the table, quietly listening to the gossip of the village. But the dragon never complained. It was much more interesting than living alone in a dark cave belonging to no one.

Nobody ever found out about the new watchdog either.

But there were rumors from time to time by people who declared excitedly that they had seen a lady walking a dragon after dark!

The Elf Who Almost Captured the Sun

Long ago, before the sun shone upon the earth, the sky was very dark. Few things glittered or sparkled and almost nothing was bright or shiny. Only the stars twinkled down, reflecting in the pools and lakes.

In one of the forests there lived a little elf who collected things and hid them in a hollow tree stump. He was fascinated by unusual leaves, by smooth stones, and by fireflies which he was forever chasing.

Then one day the sun appeared in the sky, and with it came the days and the nights.

The little elf was very excited when the sun shone for he had had no idea that there was so much color around him. He began collecting bright flowers and bits of silver that he found among the rocks, and sometimes when he saw a fish swimming in a pool, he would even try to catch one.

But of all the things he had, there was still something which he didn't have in his collection and it was by far the very brightest of them all. It was the sun.

One day he went out and found some of the morning dew caught in fine spider webs hanging across the ferns. These gave him an idea and he carefully collected them. Then he went down in the valley where the wood spiders were weaving their webs, and, finding the long strands hanging from tree to tree, he gathered them too.

Then he sat down in a place where the giant oak trees grew and wove a net. It took him the whole day, but when he had finished, he had the most wonderful net he had ever seen.

The next morning before the sun came up, the little elf awoke and stretched his arms and legs. Then he hurried down to the place where he had left his net.

Picking it up gently, he turned and climbed up the hill and walked far out to the very edge of the horizon. Then he climbed up behind a large boulder and waited.

After some time, the sun began to rise over the horizon. Just as its top appeared and the first pink rays of light began to fill the sky, the little elf picked up his net and, tossing it high, captured the sun!

Quickly he tied the end of the net to the bushes nearby. Then he pushed the heavy boulder down over the bushes so that the sun couldn't possibly get away.

The elf was very tired by the time he had finished. He staggered back to his home and went to sleep again. Nothing in his whole life had ever been so much work! But he was happy now because he had the brightest thing in the whole world in his collection!

But the animals of the forest were wondering what had

happened to the sun. They waited in their nests and burrows, and out in the fields, for the sun to shine and to warm the new day. But it never appeared.

Finally the owl and the alligator called the other animals together to discuss the matter.

"I overslept just waiting for it," said the rabbit.

"I'm worried about where it could have gone," said the rhino.

"Today is my birthday," said the parrot glumly. "Wouldn't you know that it would never show up for that?"

"Well, the only thing to do is to go look for it," chirped the blue jay.

"Where should we look?" asked the field mouse. "You know the world is a very big place."

The others agreed that to go out to find the sun might be harder than anything they had ever done before.

"I can fly out and look for it," said the owl. "My eyes are very good for things like this."

So the others waited and talked in low voices about how the sun must have gotten lost, while the owl flew out over the treetops in search of it.

The owl was gone for a very long time. Some of the animals had even gone back to bed by the time he returned, breathless and very excited.

"Did you see it?" the animals asked.

"Where is it?" asked some of them.

"Does it look the same?" asked the squirrel.

"Its light didn't go out, I hope," whispered a worried turtle as he came out of his shell.

"I've seen it. It's looking just as it always does. But it's caught in a net out on the edge of the horizon," said the owl sadly, "and I couldn't set it free because there is a boulder holding the net down."

The animals looked from one to another.

"Who would trap the sun in a net?" asked the blue jay.

Everyone became silent.

23

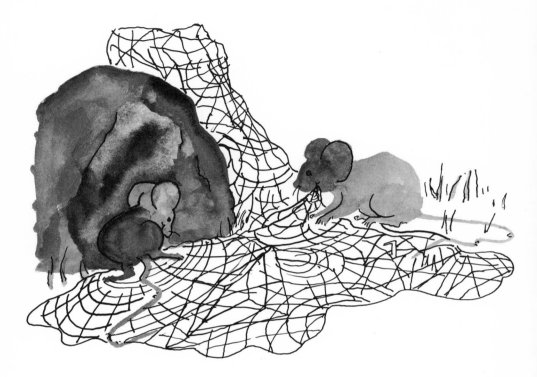

Then the field mice said, "We'll go and chew it free. A sun shouldn't be held down like that. We need it in the sky to give us all light."

Everyone agreed and the mice started off.

"Don't forget, now," the owl called after them. "Run as far as you can to the edge of the horizon, and that's the place."

So the mice ran and ran and ran and then they ran a little bit longer. In fact, they ran as far as they could right up to the edge of the horizon.

There was the sun! Round and shining brightly just down over the last mountaintop.

Quickly they scrambled forward to the place where the net was held tightly under the boulder.

"You nibble from that side, and I'll nibble from this," said one of the mice.

So they began and it took them some time.

Finally they managed to eat right through the net and the sun moved away from the mountaintop and floated up into the sky!

When the mice returned to their friends, the sun was already high up in the sky, warming the day and shedding light everywhere.

The animals were happy again and the owl decided that from this time on he would watch throughout the night so that no one would ever try to trap the sun again.

But there really never has been any problem, because the little elf was so tired out after all that climbing up to the horizon and pushing the boulder down that he has overslept every morning since.

How the Sheep
Lost His Tail

A herd of sheep lived on a farm in a part of the world not found on any map. They grazed, so the story goes, out on the edge of a lake which spread from their farmland to a great forest where the wild boars slept.

They were the first sheep ever known in those parts, and at that time they had long woolly tails. The farmer who owned them proudly showed the sheep off to visitors passing through the countryside, often telling the story of how they came to lose their tails.

The tails were of hardly any use. Bugs and fleas liked them. Sometimes the wool would grow so thick that the tails could hardly be seen. They caught in the bushes and it would take hours before the farmer came and untangled them.

One day when the farmer was out fixing the roof on his barn, the sheep, who should have been up on the side of the hill nearby, wandered out along the shores of the lake. The green leaves of the tall bushes hid the sheep from sight and, as they were intently grazing, they didn't see how close they were getting to the dangerous forest.

Now, about this time, a family of boars were out rooting in a swamp just off the lake shore, and when they heard someone coming, they jumped up and ran into the forest to hide.

This woke up a wolf who had been sleeping in the only sunny spot in the forest. The wolf was trying to remember his dream, when the boar family ran right in front of his nose.

When he saw the boar family, the wolf smiled broadly.

27

This would be a day for a feast. No wolf would turn down a dinner of tasty boar!

As the littlest boar jumped past the wolf, the great animal leaped out from his hiding place and grabbed the boar by the foot. The littlest boar squealed and squealed!

Quickly, the father boar and the mother boar returned to plead for the life of the little one.

"He's much too small," they cried. "Why eat him when there is a much bigger animal coming through the forest in a moment?"

"A much bigger animal?" asked the wolf.

"Oh, yes, very much bigger," replied the father boar.

"And tastier!" added the mother boar.

"What is it?" asked the wolf.

"Well, we didn't actually see it, but we heard it coming and that's why we were running," the boars told him.

It was true that the little boar wasn't fat enough for a fine dinner yet and the wolf could always get to him later on if he really tried. This new animal coming into the forest? The wolf was so curious about it that he had to go and see it.

So he let the little boar go. Then he crept out of the forest very quietly, and crouching behind the pines and bushes, he waited. He heard the sound of someone brushing against the branches of the trees, walking slowly.

The wolf's curiosity got the better of him and he stood up and looked out over the bushes to see what it was.

Then he saw the long-tailed sheep!

Three of them were busily eating along the edge of the lake.

Just at that moment, one of the sheep saw the wolf.

"The wolf is here!" he cried.

The sheep became very frightened. It was too far back to the farmer's yard and they couldn't run as fast as a wolf!

The wolf leaped out of the bushes. The sheep did the only thing that they could do in such an emergency! They leaped into the lake.

The wolf, however, was still faster than the last sheep, and as they all splashed into the water, he caught the sheep's tail between his teeth and held it tightly.

"Help! Help!" cried the sheep. But the others were floating out into the middle of the lake. Then, as the wolf pulled on the sheep's tail, it broke off! Quickly, the sheep swam out into the deeper water.

Late in the afternoon, the farmer got down off the barn roof and, noticing that the sheep had gone from the hillside, decided to go and look for them. To his great surprise, he saw that they were all floating toward him from the other side of the lake!

But when they reached the shore, they were unable to get out of the lake, for the water had soaked into their wool and made them too heavy.

The farmer ran down to pull them out, but they were too heavy even for him. He ran to the barn and got his horse. Then, returning to the sheep, he placed a rope around the neck of each sheep and pulled it ashore. As the last one came out he saw that its tail was broken off and he realized that something had tried to catch it.

That evening, he sheared the heavy wet wool off all the sheeps' backs and he also clipped off their long tails.

The sheep were so frightened by their narrow escape from the wolf that they learned two lessons that day.

Never did they wander over to the other side of the lake again, and never did they want to have their long woolly tails anymore.

The Lazy Boy
Who Lost the Cheeses

There once was a lazy boy who lived with his aunt on a farm high up in the mountains where the clouds sometimes drift among the trees. He was a boy who loved to daydream and it seemed to his aunt that he could never remember half the chores that he was supposed to do on the farm. She would always have to remind him to do them.

During the week the aunt made cheeses, and every Saturday she and her nephew would take them to the marketplace in the village at the foot of the mountains, to sell them.

It was easy to walk down the mountain but it took a long time to come back up, and sometimes when the aunt didn't feel well, they would go very slowly.

"My toes hurt," she would say, and they would stop to sit and rest awhile. The boy didn't mind because he thought that sitting was more fun than walking.

One Saturday the aunt's toes hurt her so much that she couldn't go with the boy to the marketplace. So she wrapped the cheeses up tightly and marked them with the prices that she expected to get for them.

"My feet aren't what they used to be," she said. "I'd make it down to the marketplace all right, but I'd never make it back up the hill. So I want you to take special care today because I'm going to send you alone. Mind, now, don't be daydreaming!"

The boy promised that he wouldn't, and then he waved his cap in the air and said good-bye.

He had not traveled far, however, when he had an accident. He was just coming around the bend in the road and heading straight down the mountainside when the bag fell open and the cheeses bounced out and rolled down the hill.

"Well," he thought, "it's too much work to go running after those cheeses. I'll just let them roll themselves to the marketplace and I'll have a better time of walking, that's for sure." He even opened his bag and let the others out.

"Hurry," he called, "don't be late. Catch up with the first ones."

When all the cheeses had rolled out of sight, he took his time going down the hill. He picked a few flowers along the road and then he investigated a bird's nest that he had seen in a willow tree, and finally, when the sun became too warm, he lay down in the field and slept a little.

He arrived in the village about noontime and he went

directly to the marketplace. There he saw all the people busily selling their goods and he looked everywhere for his cheeses. But it was obvious that no one had them.

So he sat down to think about what might have happened to them.

"Maybe they just haven't arrived yet," he said to himself hopefully. So he waited until the sun had gone down, but the cheeses never came.

Then he began asking everyone in the marketplace if they had seen his cheeses. The answers were all the same —

"No . . . " "Nope . . . " And "Not while I was here. . . ."

Then the boy started walking back through the village asking everyone he met. Some of the people looked a bit worried for him, while others only laughed. But the answers were all no. They had not seen his cheeses.

Finally the boy came to the foot of the mountain at the edge of the village. Not once in that long walk had he met anyone who had seen the cheeses.

He was becoming worried. He could hear his aunt's voice crying at him when he got home. It wasn't a pleasant thought. He tried to think of some other place the cheeses could have gone.

Then he remembered that halfway up the mountain there was a fork in the road, a place where another road came to meet the one he had walked down. This road went over to the other side of the mountain to another village.

"Of course," he said to himself. "They must have rolled down to the other village. I will go there and find them."

He hitched a ride for part of the way on a farmer's wagon, and part of the way he walked, and much of the time he just sat down to rest and to think about his problem. Finally, he arrived at the other village.

"Have you seen any cheeses rolling around?" he asked the people in the marketplace.

"No, not today," came the answers every time.

So the lazy boy who didn't want to carry his cheeses to

the marketplace had to go home and tell his aunt how he lost them.

That night when it was very late and only the owls were cooing at the bats in the trees, the boy walked into the farmyard, very, very sadly indeed.

His aunt had been sitting up on the front steps with a candle burning.

"Did you sell them all?" she asked.

The boy didn't answer.

"What took you so long? You didn't lose the money, did you?"

Then the boy bowed his head and told her how he let the cheeses roll down the mountainside.

At first, his aunt was going to send him to bed without his supper. Then she was going to give him a licking with a big stick that she kept in the shed.

But when she saw how sad he was, she gave him a couple of cookies and sent him off to the barn to sleep with the cat.

Some days after that, word passed up and down the mountain road that the field mice in the area were getting so fat that they could hardly squeeze themselves into their holes.

A Trick Well Played

The sun shone brightly overhead and the heat of the day was smothering. No wind rustled the leaves, and the flowers hung their heads along the path to the river.

Four rabbits, out looking for strawberries, stopped to listen to the river bubbling along below the rocks where they now stood.

"That must be the coolest place in world," remarked one.

"I wish I were a fish," said another.

"A fish!" cried the third rabbit. "I can think of a lot of things that I'd rather be than a fish!"

"Just long enough to cool off, I mean," answered the rabbit who had wanted to be a fish.

"If you were a fish you wouldn't be able to hop in the big forest," said one.

"And you wouldn't be able to hear things coming from far away, or visit the berry patches," said another.

"And you couldn't join us in playing tricks on the other animals," replied the third.

"True," agreed the little rabbit. "I'd be wet all day, too. But I was thinking that it might be cooler down there than it is up here."

"Well," said one little rabbit, "we could go over to the forest and get out of the sun. I'm sure that it's cooler there."

So they hopped along the path, over some rocks and through a meadow where the sun was scorching hot, and into the thick green forest. It was very cool inside.

Just as they were about to sit down among the ferns and

pussy-willow bushes they heard someone coming. Quickly they hid in among the leaves and waited.

A lion came trotting along, talking to himself.

"Now, there is a good place to take a nap," he said. "I've been chasing everybody all morning and I ought to rest and get my energy back." With that he lay down in a shallow hole covered with pine needles and closed his eyes.

When the rabbits, who had watched him, were sure that he was fast asleep, they hopped out of the bushes and returned to the edge of the forest.

"Did you see what he did?" cried one. "He lay right down in the very place that I was going to take a nap myself!"

"I've never seen him before," said another. "I wonder where he came from?"

"He talks to himself. I suppose he has no friends," remarked the third rabbit.

"Well, if he chases everybody, I should think not!" agreed the fourth.

"Let's play a trick on him," suggested the first rabbit.

"What kind of trick?" they all asked at once.

"Well, the four of us are pretty strong if we all work together," the first rabbit went on.

"Oh yes!"

"Certainly!"

"Very strong!" the answers came back.

"Then let's pick up the lion while he's asleep and carry him out to the hill where the other rabbits are having their picnic."

"Pick up the lion!!" they gasped.

"I don't feel that strong!" whispered one.

"We'll pick up the lion and take him to the hill. When he wakes up we will pretend that we have invited him to the picnic."

"Maybe he'll chase us," said one, rolling his eyes a little nervously.

"I think he will be too surprised to think of that," said

36

the first. "Besides, the bramblebushes are nearby and he can't come there."

After much talk and many suggestions they all decided that they would play the trick.

Very quietly they tiptoed back into the forest to the place where the lion lay fast asleep.

At first, it was quite difficult to lift him. Then they took two old tree branches and rolled them under him, and when they were quite sure that he wouldn't fall off, they lifted the branches. The lion was not too heavy but was long and bony, and when they picked him up, they had to be careful not to let his tummy drag.

Eventually they managed to move forward through the forest and out onto the hilltop where the other rabbits were nibbling at the clover leaves.

When the other rabbits saw the lion they were quite up-

set and some of them jumped into the bramblebushes. Gently, the four set the lion down on the grass, and they quickly told the others about the trick they were playing. The lion was still snoring with his forelegs crossed as they pulled the tree branches out from under him.

Finally the lion awakened and opened his eyes. When he saw all the rabbits hopping around him, he couldn't believe his eyes!

"Am I dreaming?" he roared with surprise.

"Oh, no," said one of the four rabbits who had carried him up the hill. "You have been here with us all afternoon. We tried not to disturb you when you took your nap."

"You promised us that you would show us how to fish," said another rabbit.

"I did?" The lion was astonished at that.

The other rabbits nodded in agreement.

"Well, then, we had better go down to the river," the lion growled, a little disconcerted. He got up and stretched. The rabbits hopped along behind him as he trotted down to the water's edge.

"Stand back, everyone," the lion called out. "I must not be distracted when I catch fish."

The river bubbled and gurgled forward and the rocks which came up to the riverbank were all slippery and wet. The lion took a few steps forward but just as his paw swept the water, he lost his balance and slid head over heels into the river.

The rabbits couldn't keep from laughing.

When the lion came up out of the water he was growling to himself. The rabbits saw that he might chase them at any moment. They all turned and quickly hopped up the hill.

The lion started after them. But before he could reach them, they had all jumped into the bramblebushes and were safe.

The lion sat down and shook his fur.

The sun was warm and he thought that he might as well take another nap and dry out.

The lion closed his eyes and after a while he began to snore loudly. The four rabbits came back and gently rolled the old tree branches up under him again.

Quietly, they picked him up and carried him back over the hilltop and into the forest to the place where they had found him.

It was getting darker and they had to be more careful along the path, but finally they came to the shallow place and they set him down gently.

When they had made certain that his paws were back in the same position, with his forelegs crossed, they hopped away.

Some time after that, when the sun had gone down and the mosquitoes were flitting up from their hiding places, the lion awoke.

He was terribly surprised to find himself back on the pine needles in the forest. Then he thought about all the rabbits and his trying to fish and their laughing at him and he decided that it must have been one bad dream.

"It's a good thing for them that it was a dream," he growled to himself, "because nobody would dare to tease a lion!"

The rabbits were by now on the other side of the forest and telling everyone they met about the fine trick that they had played on the lion.

Solving an Elf Problem

In the spring, after the rains had ended and the summer was almost on its way, a man and his pet bear liked to walk through the towns and the countryside.

Together they would make the journey. The man would knock on doors and tap on windows, asking the people if they might like to see the bear.

It was an exciting event for everyone, and the people fed the man and gave the bear some old bones. They would talk with the man late into the evenings about how strong the bear was, asking if he ever bit anyone, and if it was true that he slept all winter.

Children were always told to stand back and not to get too close, and fine ladies usually looked on from open windows.

The man had taught the bear a few tricks, and the animal could sit up, roll over, do a complete somersault, and last but not least, he would dance with the man. That always brought the evenings to a close with a great deal of squealing from the children and the fine ladies.

If the days were warm, the man might thank everyone for the good food and the visit, and then, taking his bear, he would go out into the night and they would journey on to the next village or farmhouse.

If the rains had drifted over the mountains and the ground was still wet, the people would make a place for him and his bear to sleep in the barn on sweet-smelling hay.

The man would call to his bear to wake up on those mornings, and very early, as the sun was rising on the horizon, they would start off down the road.

Now it happened that a certain farmer and his wife were having a great deal of trouble with a playful elf, who wouldn't leave them alone.

Elves had been known to be troublesome long ago, but lately they were quite polite and never really left their tiny homes in the forest. But this one didn't have an elf family of his own, and at times he became lonely, and once while wandering around the countryside singing songs to himself, he happened to pass this very farm.

He took a look in the barn and said "Boo!" to all the animals (which upset the chickens and made the rooster's tail feathers wilt, to say nothing about the impression he left on the pig), and with a good brisk walk along the eaves of the farmhouse, which made a tinny sound that echoed into the night, he decided that he liked the place enough to stay on.

That was when all the trouble came to the farmer and his wife. The elf would push the doors shut when they had been opened for air, or he would put a frog in the drinking water in the well, or if things were just too quiet for him in the middle of the night, he might climb up into the chimney and make the most terrible noises that would resound throughout the house with a hollow, ghostly boom.

The poor farmer's wife was losing her charming personality, for which she was famous, and was holding on to the last shreds of her good temper, when the man and the bear appeared at the farmhouse door. The man asked if she and her husband would like to watch his bear do a few tricks.

The farmer politely told the man that although they would like a little entertainment and that he was sure that the bear was very talented, he and his wife were moving away from the farm that evening because of the elf's troublesome tricks, and at the moment they were busy packing.

Then they told the man about the trouble that they were having with the elf.

42

The man listened carefully and the bear cuffed at the flies that had come from the barn to inspect him and he scratched a lot.

"Why don't you let me and my bear rest for the night in your house?" asked the man. "Certainly if you are about to leave, it will do no harm to allow us to be your visitors for the night. I think that we can help you."

"That's a fine idea!" said the farmer immediately. "You may be just the surprise that is needed to end this matter."

The farmer's wife looked at the bear and smiled.

So it was agreed that the man and the bear would sleep in the farmhouse that night and the farmer and his wife would go to stay at a neighboring farm.

After dark, the man lit a fire in the fireplace. The bear lay down quietly next to his chair.

The man opened a tobacco pouch and, filling his pipe, began to smoke it.

Soon the elf appeared.

He was carrying a bag with him and he stepped up in front of the man.

"Do you mind if I share the fire with you?" he asked.

"Not at all," answered the man. "Be my guest."

So the elf sat down and, opening his sack, brought out a long-legged toad and leaned over the fire to toast it.

Then he ate it.

"Would you like a toad?" he asked.

"No, thank you," said the man.

Then the elf took another toad from his sack and he toasted that one, and ate it, too.

"Would your dog like a toad?" he asked.

"No," said the man. "It is better to let him sleep. He has been walking all day."

"Well," said the elf laughingly, "dogs are usually cowards about toads anyway. I've never known a dog that could catch one."

"Mine could," answered the man, "but he's sleeping now."

"I want to see him catch a toad!" insisted the elf.

"I wouldn't bother him if I were you," said the man.

But the elf just couldn't resist teasing the sleeping "dog." He reached into his sack and pulled out a very big toad. He held it up by the legs. Then he jumped up and ran over to the bear, and waved the toad in the bear's face.

The bear leaped up and swallowed the toad, the elf and all!

The next morning the farmer and his wife returned to the farmhouse.

They were very happy that the elf problem was solved.

The farmer's wife even remarked that the bear hadn't scratched the floor too much.

So after doing a few tricks, and having their breakfast, the man and the bear waved good-bye and went on their way.

Sometimes
Around Midnight

In a land across the sea, along the old roads that lead throughout the wildest countryside where the bushes stand as tall as trees, many things still happen from time to time that people find hard to believe.

In one place it is said that the wood fairies, who are known to be very playful, will run out of the bushes around midnight and try to catch whoever is passing along the road.

When they have caught someone, the fairies form a ring around him, holding hands and singing in their strange little voices, dancing until the morning sun comes up.

More than once has a farmer come along the road searching for his cow and found it near the bushes, very weak and faint and all tuckered out with its tongue drooping on the thistle petals.

One day a little lady who lived in the village at the end of the road had taken a walk in the late afternoon with her book of riddles. She loved to read them when the sunset glowed pinkly on the pages.

But now it was late and she came along under the first stars of night, thinking that it hadn't been wise to stay out so late, as the wind hurried after her with a chill and a whisper.

It was still quite some distance to the village.

Just as she was passing the bushes where the fairies lived, a curious fellow stepped out and greeted her.

He wore a long hat with a tassel on it and he had a beautiful pair of silk wings attached to his back. His nose was a bit long, and if he were seen from the side, he would certainly be mistaken for a hummingbird of the larger variety.

Suddenly, singing came from the bushes nearby.

Then the curious fellow began to dance.

The little lady felt a strange spirit come over her! She felt like dancing too!

The singing became louder and out of the bushes stepped eleven little strange people with silken wings. They held hands and encircled the lady and the man.

"I shouldn't be dancing!" cried the lady to her partner. "I should be on my way home."

"It's too late now," answered the curious fellow, kicking his heels high in the air.

The little lady knew that she had been caught under the spell of the dancing fairies. There was no way to stop now.

Then she thought of something.

"I cannot dance with my book in hand. May I put it on a stone nearby?"

The stranger clapped his hands and the music stopped.

When the music stopped, the spell that had captured the lady stopped too.

Carefully she placed the book on the rock.

The music began again and again they began to dance.

"What is your book about?" asked the curious fellow.

"About two hundred pages long," answered the lady.

"Does it have stories about fairies in it?" asked the fellow.

"No," said the lady as she spun around to the music, "it's just a book of riddles."

The curious fellow clapped his hands again and the music stopped.

"Riddles!" exclaimed the fellow. "We love riddles!"

"This book would be too hard for you to understand," said the lady. "If you don't believe it take a look."

All the fairies forgot their singing and rushed over to look into the riddle book.

But because they weren't used to reading to themselves,

they read aloud slowly and moved their lips carefully to each word.

It took so much of their concentration that they completely forgot about the lady.

Quietly she tiptoed out of their company. When she had reached the top of the hill and could see the village ahead, she turned back to take one last look at the fairies.

There they were all huddled around the riddle book, reading together. She could just barely understand what they were saying as the words drifted across the wind.

"What steps does one take to escape a dragon?"

She smiled to herself.

"I'm putting that one into practice right now." And turning, she took giant steps into the village.

Since that time, very few cows have been captured by the fairies because, it has been said, they are still trying to solve the riddles.

Some people coming on the road at midnight still hear singing as usual, but once in a while on a very high wind little voices cry out, asking,

"When does a brook that's bubbling past
Finally become still and quiet at last?"

And if a person has never been to a lake, he may never find out the answer either.

The Fox and the Goose

One summer day in the fields of Holland, a goose was digging around the tulips for worms and grubs. A fox, trotting along the canal nearby, spied her.

The fox decided then and there that the goose would make a delicious dinner and that he would have to think of some clever way to catch her before she could fly away.

So he began to sing a little song to himself about how pretty the tulips were, and when he passed the goose, he smiled broadly and waved his tail.

"Hello, Goosey!" he called out. "A lovely day for digging in the tulips, isn't it?"

The goose looked up, quite surprised, and agreed, "Oh, yes, it is, it is."

"I see that you are doing not the best job of it, either," the fox said, smiling again. "I cannot help feeling proud of being a fox, when it comes to that."

"What do you mean?" asked the goose.

"Well, Goosey, I don't think that anyone anywhere can really dig a hole or a tunnel as well as a fox can," he teased.

"Oh?" asked the goose. "Are foxes especially proud of that?"

"Absolutely!" exclaimed the fox. "When it comes to digging a hole, even a rabbit couldn't do better."

Then he looked about the field and along the bank of the canal quickly.

"Here, let me show you," he said.

And very quickly the fox dug through the bank of the canal and made a tunnel that looked large and wide from the outside and was just a bit narrow on the inside.

The goose came over and looked at the tunnel.

"It looks fine," she said. "We geese could never dig something like that."

"Go ahead and try it," the fox said. "A tunnel like that one isn't my best of course, but it's worth trying out."

So the goose waddled in, looked around, and tried to step through. But before she had gotten halfway, she was stuck!!

"Oh dear!" exclaimed the goose. "I'm stuck and can't seem to get one feather forward!"

"Well," laughed the fox as he smacked his lips, "you must be having trouble because you are nice and fat and ready for eating."

Suddenly the goose realized the trick that the fox had played on her and she tried desperately to think how to get out of her predicament.

"Your tunnel is a very good one," she said again. "Only someone as clever as a fox could make it so well."

The fox thought he was very clever, too.

"But," said the goose, "while I could never dig a tunnel like this one, I'm sure that I can do something no fox has ever done."

"That," said the fox without a smile, "isn't very likely at all."

"If you will set me free, I'll teach it to you," the goose said.

"What is it?" asked the fox. "Maybe I already know how to do it."

"No, I'm sure you don't," answered the goose.

"Well, what is it?" asked the fox, getting very curious indeed.

"Can you fly?" asked the goose.

"No," said the fox, "I cannot do that."

"Then set me free, and I'll teach you how," said the goose.

The fox thought about it for a moment, wondering what he should do. If he could fly, he could easily catch all the birds, geese, and ducks that he wanted. And certainly, he had never heard of any other fox being able to fly.

So the fox took hold of the goose's feet and pulled her out of the tunnel.

The goose was a bit ruffled from the tight squeeze in the narrow tunnel but now she was free. She made up her mind that the fox would never trick her again.

"Climb on my back," said the goose, "and I will show you how easy it is to fly."

So the fox climbed up on the goose's back and the goose flew up into the air.

Up, up, up they went, and the fox was just getting used to being up so high when the goose shook her feathers and the fox rolled off!

He fell straight down, but it happened that he was saved from being hurt because he landed in a pile of hay.

The goose flew down over his head and landed in front of him.

"Wasn't that fun?" she asked. "Did you like it?"

"Well, it takes a little getting used to," replied the fox, "but I suppose that I could learn to like it in time."

"It's a matter of practice," agreed the goose. "We should go up again before you forget how."

So the fox climbed on her back again.

This time the goose flew as fast as she could, and then turning into the wind, she sailed high above the clouds.

Again she shook her feathers.

The fox dropped straight down through a little puffy cloud into a lake below. He made a very big splash and was never seen again.

The goose returned to the tulip field, where she began digging for worms and grubs again.

"The fox," she thought, "has been outsmarted at his own game."

The Shopkeeper's Secret

One day when a shopkeeper was out taking a walk on the road leading away from his village, he happened to see something in the bushes that glittered in the afternoon sunlight. Being of a curious nature, he stepped off the road to have a closer look, and was astonished at the sight that met his eyes as he parted the leaves.

There before him was a chest that was filled to the brim with pearls and golden coins! Almost as soon as he had realized his good fortune, he began to worry about his neighbors. They would certainly be jealous if they heard about his great luck. He would have to be very careful not to let anyone know about the wonderful chest.

Just then, he looked up and saw, coming along the road, a fellow who was known throughout the valley for never being able to keep a secret. The fellow waved to him as he came closer.

Quickly the shopkeeper thought of a plan. The chest was much too heavy for him to carry by himself, so he would get the fellow to help him, yet make sure that his neighbors in the village did not find out about the chest.

"I wonder," he said, as the fellow came up to him, "I wonder if you would be so kind as to help me guard my chest of pearls and coins? It is too heavy for me to carry, and I must go to the village to get a wheelbarrow. Will you sit here and guard it while I'm gone?"

At this, the man was very excited, and he said, "Oh, yes, I'll be happy to help! How wonderful! How did you find the chest?"

"Well," said the shopkeeper, "I don't mind telling you, but I wouldn't want the news to get around, so I'll have to ask you to keep it a secret."

"Oh, I won't tell a soul!" the fellow replied.

"Well," said the shopkeeper, "I was just walking along thinking of nothing special when I heard someone crying. When I turned to look over here in the bushes, I saw a tiny little star caught in the branches."

"A star?" cried the man. "How amazing!"

"I came over to see it better," said the shopkeeper, "and just as I approached, a little Princess stepped out."

"Ooooohh!" cried the fellow. "Why don't things like that happen to me? What did you do then?"

"I was quite surprised, of course. But we talked a bit and the Princess told me that she lived in the star, and that some-how during the night it had become tangled in the branches of this little tree," said the shopkeeper.

"Where is it now? I don't see it," remarked the fellow.

"She asked me to throw it back up into the sky. So I did," said the shopkeeper. "And when I looked down at my feet, there was this chest of coins and pearls!"

"Marvelous!" cried the fellow. "It must be your reward!"

"Marvelous, indeed," agreed the shopkeeper. "You can see why it should be kept a secret."

"Of course," cried the fellow. "I won't tell a soul!"

"Thank you," said the shopkeeper. "Now I must go and get a wheelbarrow. Will you stay here and guard the chest while I'm gone? I won't be long."

"Oh, yes," replied the man. "I'll be glad to help." And as he said this he kept looking up to the sky in the hope of seeing the little star where the Princess lived.

When the shopkeeper got to his shop, he went and fetched several items and put them into a bag. He took five fish and twenty-two cookies and one whole big salami. Then he put the bag into the wheelbarrow and started back.

When he came to the bridge just outside of the town, he

took out his salami and tied it to the end of a string and dangled it over the side of the bridge into the water below. Then he continued on until he came to a tree by the road. Here, he took the cookies out and carefully hung them on the branches. Then he went on and when he had almost reached the spot where the fellow was waiting with the chest, he took out the five fish and laid them end to end across the road.

Finally he came up to the man waiting with the chest, and together they lifted the chest into the wheelbarrow and covered it with the empty bag. Then they started back toward the village.

First they came upon the five fish.

"Look!" cried the fellow. "Five fish laid end to end across the road! I've never seen that before! How could fish get out here on the road?"

"Oh, it's quite common for fish to take walks," remarked the shopkeeper.

"Oh?" said the man. "I've never heard of that!"

After some time they passed the tree with the cookies hanging from the branches.

"Look!" the fellow cried again. "Cookies hanging in the tree!"

"Oh, yes," remarked the shopkeeper. "It was raining cookies this morning. Didn't you notice it?"

"Raining cookies!" cried the man. "What a curious day!"

Then, as they crossed the bridge, it was quite easy to see the large salami dangling on a string in the water below.

"I've never seen that before!" cried the fellow in great fright.

"Oh," said the shopkeeper, "that must belong to the giant who comes out of the mountains at night to fish. He probably forgot his fishing pole."

"Fishing with a salami? A giant from the mountains?" cried the poor fellow. "It's all too strange to think about!"

It had grown dark by the time they got back to the village, and when they had lifted the chest into the shopkeeper's house, the shopkeeper thanked the fellow very much for helping him. He gave him a cake from his shop and told him good night.

The next day, bright and early, the fellow was in the marketplace. He didn't look very well because he had not slept at all the night before. Someone asked him why he was yawning so much.

"Well, I had such an exciting day yesterday that I just couldn't close my eyes all night," he replied.

"What did you do?" someone asked.

"I helped the shopkeeper carry his chest of gold home!" said the fellow, who couldn't keep a secret.

"Gold!" the other men cried with amazement.

"Yes, gold coins, and pearls, too," answered the fellow.

"We didn't know the shopkeeper was rich," said the men.

"He wasn't, but he is now. The Princess who lives in the star gave it to him."

"Princess? Who lives *where*?" someone asked.

"Oh, I know. I had a hard time believing it myself," said the fellow, "but that wasn't the only thing that was strange. When we came back to the village we met five fish taking a walk. Then we saw a salami that the giant left on his fishing line. That's probably because it was raining cookies."

Quietly, the other men in the marketplace moved away from the fellow and went about their work. When the shopkeeper came out, no one asked him about the chest of coins. So it was a well-kept secret. The shopkeeper knew that his chest was safe. And one day the fellow told the shopkeeper that it was a pity that people didn't believe the truth when they heard it.

Robert Sargent, author and illustrator of a number of children's books, lived in Europe for many years, where he conducted his own television program for children. The recipient of many awards for his paintings and book jackets, Mr. Sargent now lives in New York City.